This is Fireman Fergus. He is a
brave firefighter and he has a good
head for heights. Fireman Fergus
has a cat called Tibbles to whom he
tells all his Fireman's adventures.

A catalogue record for this book is available from the British Library

Published by Ladybird Books Ltd
80 Strand London WC2R 0RL
A Penguin Company

8 10 9

© LADYBIRD BOOKS LTD MMI

LADYBIRD and the device of a Ladybird are trademarks of Ladybird Books Ltd

Little Workmates

Fireman Fergus

by Mandy Ross

illustrated by Emma Dodd

Ladybird

"Leaping ladders! What a storm last night!" Fireman Fergus said to Tibbles one morning. "Did you hear the wind howling?"

Just as Fireman Fergus got to work, the emergency bell rang,

"DING-Â-LING-A-LING!"

"Leaping ladders! A tree blew down in the storm and it's blocking the road," said Fireman Fergus.

Nee-naw! Nee-naw!

Fireman Fergus drove
the fire engine through
Story Town, but...

"Leaping ladders!
A traffic jam,"
groaned
Fireman Fergus.

Nee-naw!

"Let us through!"

The fire engine squeezed
past Builder Bill's truck...
and Mrs Farmer's tractor...
and PC Polly's motorbike.

At last Fireman Fergus reached the tree.

"Leaping ladders! It's huge!" he said.

"Look! There's a nest," said PC Polly. "Some baby birds are stuck there."

Fireman Fergus climbed up his longest ladder...

He reached the nest and tucked it carefully into his pocket. Then he climbed down.

PC Polly looked after
the baby birds.

"Well done,
Fireman Fergus,"
she said. "Now,
what about
this tree?"

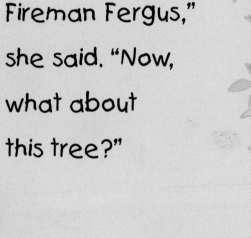

Fireman Fergus fixed a chain from the fire engine round the tree. He started the engine, but...

"Leaping ladders! This tree won't budge!"

"We're coming to help!"
called Builder Bill.
He drove over in his
truck, followed
by Mrs Farmer
in her tractor.

Fireman Fergus
fixed on
more chains.

"Ready, steady, HEAVE!" shouted Fireman Fergus.

Together, they heaved the tree off the road.

"Leaping ladders, we've done it!"

Fireman Fergus drove the fire engine back to the fire station, ready for work the next day.

"It's time I went home for my tea," he said.

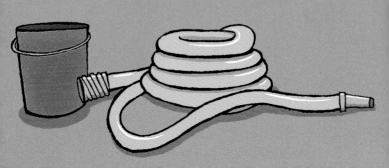

"That was a good day's work," he told Tibbles. "But leaping ladders! I hope there won't be another storm tonight!"

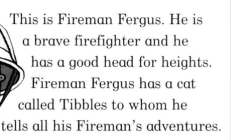

This is Fireman Fergus. He is a brave firefighter and he has a good head for heights. Fireman Fergus has a cat called Tibbles to whom he tells all his Fireman's adventures.

This is Nurse Nancy. She is always neat and tidy and she works very hard looking after the patients at Story Town Hospital.

This is Builder Bill with his yellow hard hat. Builder Bill loves to whistle. He is a very good builder, and his houses never fall down.